MY VERY FIRST
RUMPELSTILTSKIN
STORYBOOK

Retold by Rochelle Larkin
Illustrated by Nan Brooks

Copyright © MCMXCIV Playmore Inc., Publishers
and Waldman Publishing Corp. New York, New York.
Printed in China

Once upon a time there lived a miller who had a beautiful daughter. He was very proud, and he wanted her to be much more than a miller's daughter. So he went to the king and told him he had a daughter who could spin straw into gold.

Now, the king was as greedy as the miller
was proud, so they struck a bargain. The miller's
daughter came to live at the castle, where she
was put into a room heaped with straw. "Spin
this into gold," said the king, "and you'll be
queen. If not, you will lose your life."

The miller's daughter was left alone. All night long she cried and cried. She could barely spin flax into cloth, let alone straw into gold.

Suddenly, a little man flew into the room. "Why are you crying?" he asked in his funny squeaky voice.

"Because the king wants me to spin all this straw into gold by morning and I don't know how," she said and started crying again.

"What will you give me to do it?"
the little man asked.

"I have very little," the miller's daughter
answered. "But you can have this ring."

"It's not much, but I'll do it," said the little man.

When the king came in the next morning and saw the room piled high with gold, he was both pleased and astonished.

"Unbelievable," he said. "You must do it again." And the miller's daughter was put into an even bigger room with even more straw.

Again, the strange little man came to her aid.

"Help me," she pleaded, "or I will lose my life."

"When you are queen," said the little man, "and you will be, you will give me your firstborn child."

"Yes, yes, anything you want," said the miller's daughter, thinking only to save her life.

When the king saw all the gold that had been spun that night, he married the miller's daughter. Now she was the queen.

When a baby prince was born to them, the king and queen were as happy as could be. All of the queen's fears were forgotten until one morning when the strange little man flew in at the window to remind her of her promise.

"Oh no!" cried the queen. "You can't take my baby from me. You mustn't!" But nothing she offered him made the little man change his mind.

At last he gave in. "If you can guess my name in three days," he said, "you may keep the child. But three days, mind you." And with that, out the window he flew.

The queen was more frightened than before. She couldn't tell the king about the gold, and couldn't bear the thought of losing her child.

She sent for the captain of the castle. "You must search high and low," she said. "Find me the strangest names you can."

The captain searched through all the northern
part of the kingdom and brought a list to the queen.

The morning came, and with it the little man
flew through the window again.

"Well, do you have it?" he demanded.

The queen began. "Is your name Maxey, Jaxey, or Gullfaxi?" she asked.

"No!" roared the little man.

"Is it Kenny, Lenny, or Benny?" asked the queen.

"No!" shouted the little man, "and you'd better have better names tomorrow!"

The captain went out again, searching the
southern part of the kingdom. He listened carefully
to all the names he heard and wrote them all down.

Next morning, the queen was ready for the little man.

"Is your name Ingnozel, Bingnozel, or Stringnozel?" she asked desperately.

"No, no, and no!" the little man screamed. "You'll never guess!"

The captain went out to search the middle part of the kingdom, but all the names he heard were names he had heard before. He was about to go to the queen with this sad news when a strange noise caught his ear.

Down at the entrance to a nearly hidden cave, he saw the strange little man doing a little dance and singing to himself.

"Oh, tomorrow the child I shall claim," he sang as he hopped about on one foot, "sure as Rumpelstiltskin is my name!"

The captain wrote it down
and hurried back to the queen.

When he described the little man,
the queen knew she was saved.

Next morning, in he flew.
"Give me the child," he said to the queen.

"Is your name John?" she asked with a smile.

"Of course not!" he snapped. "What's unusual about the name John?"

"Is it Peter?" asked the queen.

"Give me the child!" the little man shouted.

The queen smiled again.
"Is it Rumpelstiltskin?" she asked.
"You guessed! You guessed!" the little man
shouted, stamping with both feet on the floor.

In fact, he stamped so hard that the floor opened right up and swallowed him whole.

Rumpelstiltskin disappeared completely. He was never seen again.

The king, the queen, and the little prince lived happily ever after.